W9-CMU-833

MARC BROWN

Volunteer of the Year

Francine waved to Arthur.

"Over here," she called. "Did you hear about Muffy's award?"

"What award?" asked Arthur.

"The Senior Center's Junior Volunteer of the Year Award," Muffy said.

"For the young person who best demonstrates the spirit of giving," Prunella read aloud.

"I'm going to win," said Muffy.

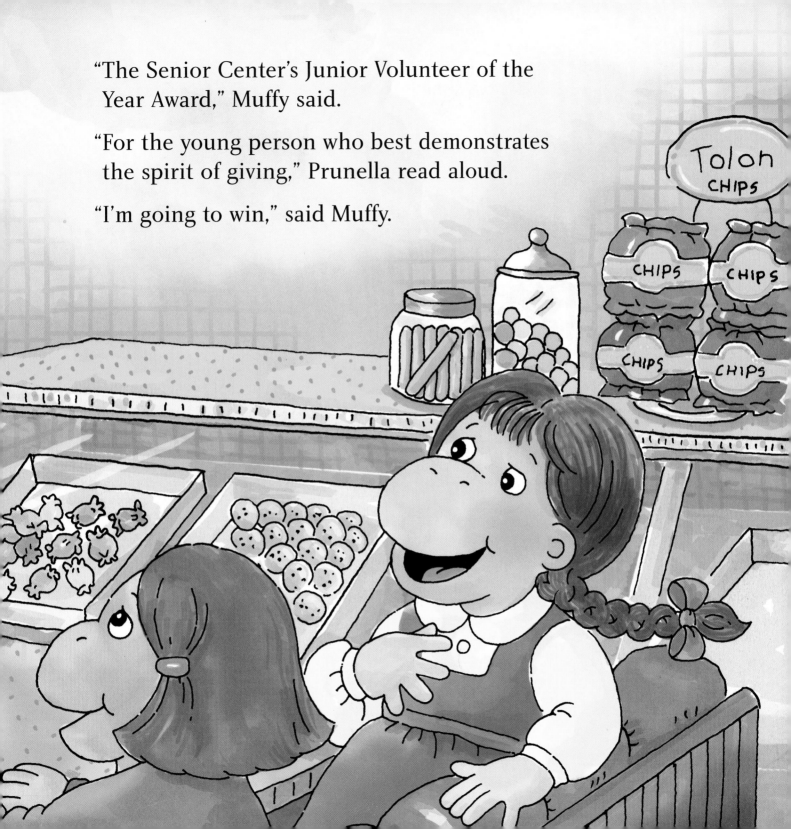

On her way home, Muffy stopped at a nursery.

"I'll take 10 of the blue plants and 15 of those pink things," said Muffy. "Please deliver these to the Senior Center this afternoon with my note."

Later that day, Arthur helped his dad serve refreshments at the Senior Center.

The plants Muffy had sent were piled up out back.

"Wow! That's a lot of plants," said Arthur.

"It certainly is," said Mrs. Runyon.

"Need some help planting them?" asked Arthur.

"That would be wonderful," she said.

Three months later, the plants were in full bloom for the Fourth of July picnic.

"I'd like my burger rare," said Miss Stine.

Just then, Muffy arrived. "Here are some picnic things," she said. "And don't forget to let everybody know I brought them!"

"Looks like you've got some decorating to do,"
said Mr. Evans. "Let me help."

Mr. Evans helped Arthur hang the streamers.

Before long, everything was red, white, and blue.

"Let's have some lemonade," said Mr. Evans.

"How did you get your medals?" asked Arthur.

"Haven't I already told you?" asked Mr. Evans.

"I want to hear it again," said Arthur.

At the Senior Center Crafts Fair, Arthur helped set up the booths.

"Would you help me untangle my yarn, Arthur?" asked Miss Stine.

"Sure," said Arthur.

Mrs. Runyon was showing Arthur how to
make clothespin reindeer when Muffy
came by with Prunella.

"I'll take five of everything," said Muffy.
"It's all for a very good cause."

"Wow," said Arthur. "She sure bought a lot of stuff."

"True," said Miss Stine. "But money doesn't buy everything. Like this scarf I made for you."

That winter, a big snowstorm hit Elwood City.

"Hooray!" shouted Arthur. "No school!"

"No circle time," smiled D.W.

"Finish your breakfast," said Dad.

After a morning of sledding and snowball fights, Arthur called Muffy.

"I'm going over to the Senior Center," said Arthur. "Want to come?"

"Are you kidding?" said Muffy. "It's freezing out there!"

When Arthur got to the Senior Center, he noticed that the path needed shoveling.

"Why, thank you," said Mr. Evans.

Then they all played Go Fish.

Arthur was laughing at a funny joke when a bakery truck pulled up outside.

"A delivery from a Miss Muffy Crosswire," said the man.

Everyone enjoyed the pastries after the card game.

A few weeks later, Arthur ran into Muffy at the florist shop.

"I just ordered ten dozen roses for the Senior Center," said Muffy. "So they won't forget about my contribution."

"I still have so much to do," she said. "I want to look just right for the awards ceremony tonight."

"See you there," said Arthur. "I'm helping my dad with the buffet."

That night, while Muffy was getting her hair done, Arthur listened to Mr. Ronzini's famous fish tale.

"Biggest fish ever seen..." said Mr. Ronzini. "Too bad it got away."

While Muffy took a bubble bath, Arthur played checkers with Mrs. Runyon.

"I'm going to win this time," said Arthur.

"King me," said Mrs. Runyon.

Muffy couldn't decide between "Magnificent Mango" or "Fabby Fuchsia" nail polish.

Meanwhile, at the Senior Center, Arthur helped
Mr. Evans put on his best jacket.

"How do I look?" he asked.

"Great," said Arthur.

"I'm here!" announced Muffy. "The ceremony can start."

"Thank you all for coming," the announcer began,
"and for the wonderful community support this past year."

Everyone applauded.

"Now for my favorite part of the evening," he continued.
"This year's Junior Volunteer of the Year Award goes to...
Arthur Read!"

"Arthur?" gasped Muffy. "What did he give?"

"His time," said Francine, "his friendship, and hard work."

"Way to go Arthur!" cried Miss Runyon.

"You're my hero!" shouted Miss Stine.

"You're the best!" yelled Mr. Evans.

Everyone in the audience stood up.

A photographer took Arthur's picture. "Let's see a big smile," called Mrs. Baxter, "for the Volunteer of the Year!"